First published in
North America by Annick Press 2003
Text © 2002 Meg Clibbon
Illustrations © 2002 Lucy Clibbon
Originally published by Zero to Ten Limited
(a member of the Evans Publishing Group)
© 2002 Zero to Ten Limited

Cataloging in Publication
Clibbon, Meg
Imagine you're a wizard! / text by Meg Clibbon ; illustrations by Lucy Clibbon. --
North American ed.
(Imagine this! series)
ISBN 1-55037-793-0 (bound).--ISBN 1-55037-792-2 (pbk.)
1. Wizards--Juvenile literature. I. Clibbon, Lucy II. Title. III. Series:
Clibbon, Meg. Imagine this! series.
BF1611.C55 2003   j398'.45   C2002-905210-6

Distributed in Canada and the U.S.A. by Firefly Books Ltd.
www.annickpress.com
Printed in China

Imagine you're a Wizard!

Meglin

(also known as Meg Clibbon)
has special powers, but she knows how tricky these can be if they are not properly used, so she is learning to be wise as well. She is greatly helped in this by her husband, a great magician, who helps to keep her powers under control.

Lucy Lightning

(also known as Lucy Clibbon)
is inspired by the mysterious and magical world of wizards. She once went to an enchanted castle with some real wizards where she learnt how to do magic.

We would like to dedicate this book to
two magical brothers, Harry and Max

What is a wizard?

Definition:
a wizard is someone with special
and extraordinary powers.

What do wizards look like?

There are some wizards who are young and good-looking.
There are some wizards who are old with long beards.

There are thin wizards, girl wizards, tall wizards,
chunky wizards, and little wizards.

All wizards are clever and
bossy and they love showing off.
This is why they wear such
peculiar clothes.

Becoming a wizard

You can become a wizard by working very hard at certain skills such as cooking, dancing, drama, astronomy, chemistry, and the study of nature. When you are good at all these things, you need to get yourself a pointed hat, a magic wand, a cloak, a cauldron, and a long stick. Then you need to go off and set up home in a cave somewhere and get ready to amaze everybody with your special powers.

What wizards need to learn

Cooking – Wizards do a lot of cooking in a cauldron using rather strange ingredients.

Dancing – Wizards dance around fires in special ways that impress everyone watching.

Drama – Wizards shout and throw their arms about to gain attention. Their outfits help too.

Astronomy – Wizards know all about the movement of the moon, stars, and planets.

Chemistry – If wizards did not know about the things they throw into their cauldron, it could be disastrous. (It sometimes is!)

Nature study – This is what wizards like best and it is what they are very good at.

What do wizards wear?

Magic wand

Pointed hat →

Long staff →

Beard

Pet

Magic cloak
(also good
for keeping
warm
at night)

Cauldron
(big iron
pot)

rubber boots (for muddy forests)

Equipment and accessories

In order to be a wizard you will need
some of the following equipment.

**Snack and drink
for extra energy**

Animal masks

**Rune stones
for secrets**

**Big spoon to
stir cauldron**

Dry socks

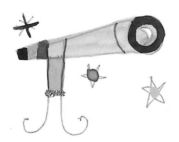

**Telescope to
look at sky**

Face paint

Big spell book

Astrolabe

Chemistry set

Herbs

Chunky pendant

Where do wizards work?

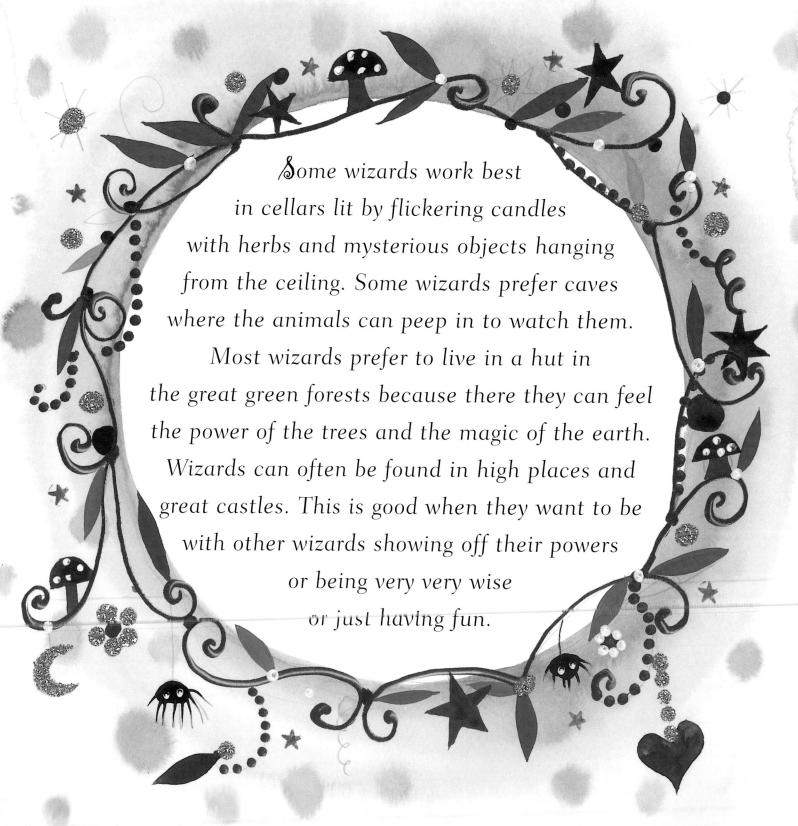

Some wizards work best
in cellars lit by flickering candles
with herbs and mysterious objects hanging
from the ceiling. Some wizards prefer caves
where the animals can peep in to watch them.
Most wizards prefer to live in a hut in
the great green forests because there they can feel
the power of the trees and the magic of the earth.
Wizards can often be found in high places and
great castles. This is good when they want to be
with other wizards showing off their powers
or being very very wise
or just having fun.

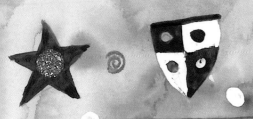

Wizard club

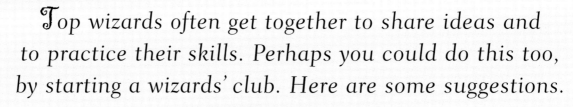

Top wizards often get together to share ideas and to practice their skills. Perhaps you could do this too, by starting a wizards' club. Here are some suggestions.

Members

You need to have a list of members.
Names are important, so perhaps your members could choose secret wizard names that only other members know. You could have secret signs too.

Password

Think of one word or a sentence that only members know. Only people who know the password can come to the meetings.

Owls hoot at midnight!

Badge

Design a badge for your club. This design can be used for the front of the hats, on the cloaks, rule books, and anything else to do with the club.

Codes

In a code you have to substitute the 26 letters of the alphabet with other letters, numbers, or marks that are known only to you and your friends.

Then you can send messages to each other without anyone else understanding. (But look after your code book!)

The easiest code is this one:

A=1	B=2	C=3	D=4	E=5	F=6	G=7
H=8	I=9	J=10	K=11	L=12	M=13	N=14
O=15	P=16	Q=17	R=18	S=19	T=20	U=21
V=22	W=23	X=24	Y=25	Z=26		

So "wizard" would be 23-9-26-1-18-4.

Or you could put a "keyword" in first like this:

A=**M**	B=**E**	C=**R**	D=**L**	E=**I**	F=**N**
G=A	H=B	I=C	J=D	K=F	L=G	M=H
N=J	O=K	P=O	Q=P	R=Q	S=S	T=T
U=U	V=V	W=W	X=X	Y=Y	Z=Z	

Why don't you try making up your own code?

Animal friends

All wizards know about animals.
They often have pet animals or birds to help them
with their work. Here are some of their favorites.

Raven – happy in cellars or
caves but must be able to fly out

Horse – needs a lot of
attention and hay but
good on journeys

Owl – for forest use only

Cat – quite happy
inside houses or caves

Mice – useful anywhere

Frog – only any good
in swampy areas

Wizards can talk to animals.
They study how animals behave and can
copy them. They like making animal masks and
pretending to be animals. By doing this,
it seems as though they turn into animals.

Can you ...

Hop like a rabbit?

Growl like a bear?

Blink like an owl?

Jump like a frog?

Curl up and go to sleep like a hedgehog?

Run like a deer?

Gallop like a horse?

Astronomy

Stargazing and studying the night sky take up
a lot of wizards' time. In the sky are millions of stars and planets.
Groups of stars are known as constellations.
The wizards use their telescopes or binoculars and star charts
to look at them all and marvel at them.
What with one thing and another, wizards don't get much sleep,
but at night, under a starry sky, when they are tired after all that
looking, they pull their pointy hats down over their ears,
wrap themselves up in their cloaks, and dream dreams.

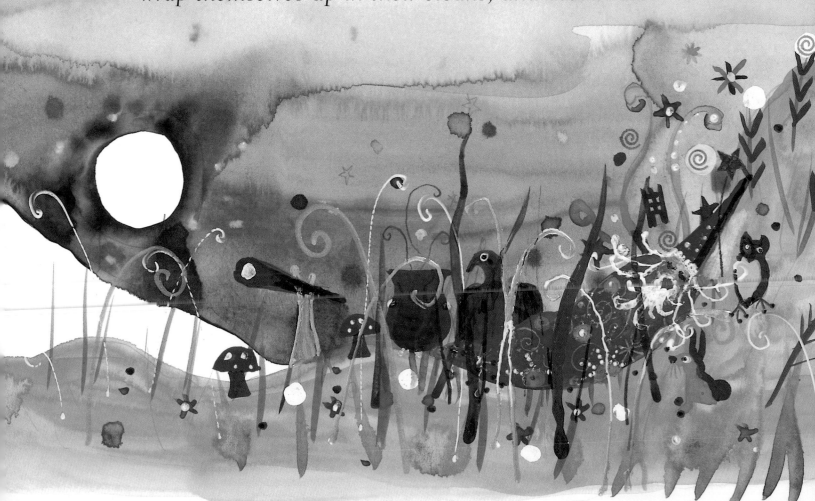

Earth watch

Because wizards love the earth and nature,
they know about weather watching and what happens to
the world at different times of the day.
They get worried if there is not enough rain or
too much rain. They know when rivers get polluted and
when trees are sad. They can warn people
and try to put things right.

Wizard history

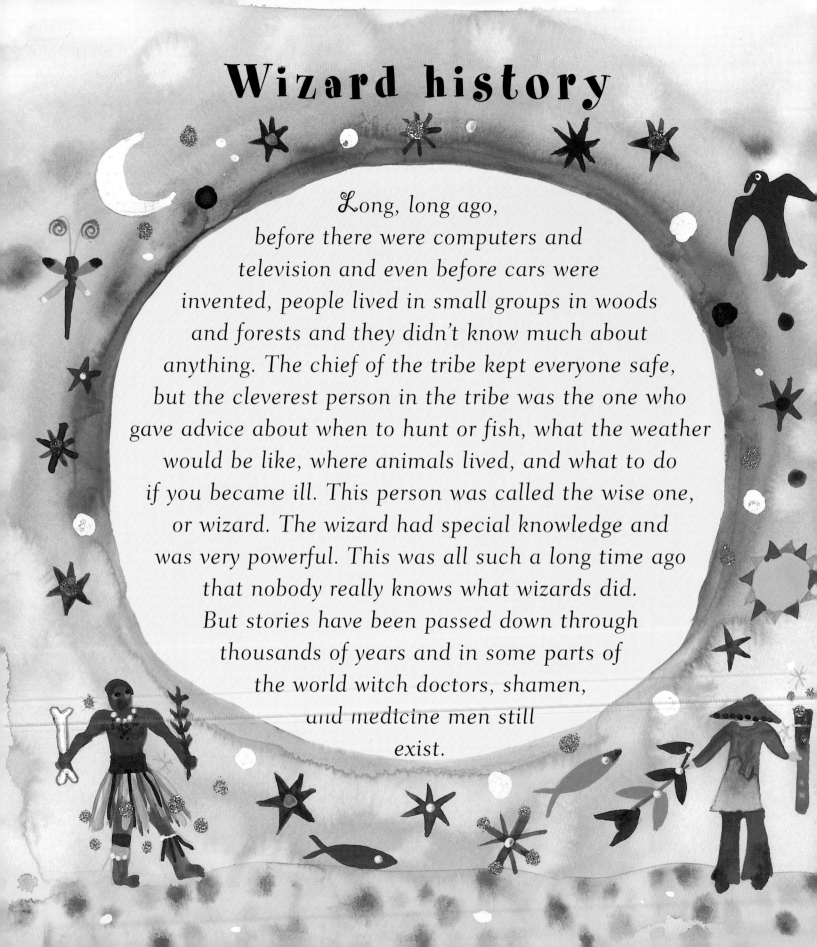

Long, long ago,
before there were computers and
television and even before cars were
invented, people lived in small groups in woods
and forests and they didn't know much about
anything. The chief of the tribe kept everyone safe,
but the cleverest person in the tribe was the one who
gave advice about when to hunt or fish, what the weather
would be like, where animals lived, and what to do
if you became ill. This person was called the wise one,
or wizard. The wizard had special knowledge and
was very powerful. This was all such a long time ago
that nobody really knows what wizards did.
But stories have been passed down through
thousands of years and in some parts of
the world witch doctors, shamen,
and medicine men still
exist.

Famous wizards

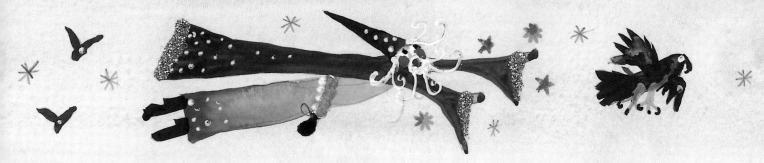

Merlin was the wizard in the legend of King Arthur.
He was very wise and very powerful. He had taught Arthur as
a boy and became his most trusted adviser. It was Merlin
who chose the knights to sit at the Round Table.
All the knights had to promise to be gentle, brave, and strong,
to do justice, to be kind to women, loyal to each other,
true in friendship, and faithful in love.
We need knights like that today!

Gandalf is the wizard in The Hobbit and
The Lord of the Rings by J.R.R. Tolkien. In The Hobbit Gandalf
gathers together a group of dwarves, joined very reluctantly by
Bilbo Baggins the hobbit, in a quest to find the treasure guarded by
the dragon Smaug far beyond the Lonely Mountains.
Gandalf is very mysterious and appears and disappears
at unexpected moments. He has a long white beard and wears
a long cloak and a tall pointed hat.

Spell books

Every wizard needs a spell book. It is best if this is very large and dusty and has very difficult words in it. The spell book proves to everyone that the wizard is really clever and can read. Can you read this spell from How to Cook Potions, *Book Four?*

Fame Flowers

Collect snapdragons in the middle of the day when the sun is hot. Boil* the flowers and seeds in a couldron with one flagon of water and a goodly lump of butter. When cool, collect the fat. Rub into the skin and you will become famous one day.

*You might need an old, wizened assistant (like a parent) to help with this.

What is a flagon? Perhaps you could look it up in a dictionary.

Wizard words

potion   wand   mystery   cauldron

wisdom   dancing   secret   astronomy

chemistry   constellation

Even very clever wizards sometimes get things wrong. A nasty explosion has scattered letters all over the place. Grab a pencil and paper and see how quickly you can write out the letters in their correct order.

dnwa

diwmos

nitoop

dlroncau

llattoenniocs

natorsomy

treesc

gincand

chtimyres

ytrmyse

Wizards at home

Bewitching web

Main bat

Special wishing hats

Wish bringers

Ivy tendrils

Glamorous bedroom

Incantation robes

Secret steps

to silent cellar

Velvet drapes

Enchanted slippers

Owl

Brooms

Broom stand

*N*obody is quite sure where wizards used to live or where they live now because their homes are protected by powerful spells.

Spider

Astrolabe

Stained glass window

Raven roost

Spell books and scrolls

Previous apprentice

Vials

Magic ravens

Philters and potions

Amulets and charms

Herbs

Cauldron

Ladle

Magic spell ingredients

Globe

Fourth mouse

Lazy cat on magic carpet

Three blind mice

Stool for apprentice

Aromatic logs

They are thought to live up twisty turning turrets in chilly, creepy castles, or in dank, dark dungeons or cold caves. Probably they prefer a cozy corner in a silent, spidery cellar like this one.

Things to do

Clothes

You can make a hat by rolling a piece of card or stiff paper into a cone. Trim, paint, and decorate it with magic emblems, such as stars.
A cloak can be made out of dark material and also trimmed with stars.

Magic wand

This is easy to make by rolling up a piece of 8.5" x 11" paper covered in glue. When it is dry, paint it.

Wizard sticks

A long wooden stick should be painted and decorated with feathers, beads, bells, and pine cones. It is important to wave it and shake it in dances and spells.

More things to do

Yog-wiz

Wizards love food. Here is a favorite treat.

Instructions:
Into tall sundae glasses
spoon layers of plain yogurt,
soft brown sugar, and fruits of the forest.
Chill, then eat.

Animal masks

These can be made out of cardboard
with cut-out eyeholes. Elastic or tape keeps
them in place. The masks should be
painted to look like animals and they are even
better if you can stick on animal fur fabric, with
details such as whiskers added later.